The Color of Veggie

By Sonia Sander

New York   London   Toronto   Sydney

An imprint of Simon & Schuster Children's Publishing Division
1230 Avenue of the Americas, New York, New York 10020
Copyright © 2006 by Big Idea, Inc.
VEGGIETALES®, character names, likenesses, and other indicia are trademarks of Big Idea, Inc.
All rights reserved. Used under license.
All rights reserved, including the right of reproduction in whole or in part in any form.
SIMON SCRIBBLES and associated colophon are trademarks of Simon & Schuster, Inc.
Manufactured in the United States of America
First Edition
2 4 6 8 10 9 7 5 3 1
ISBN-13: 978-1-4169-1786-1
ISBN-10: 1-4169-1786-1

What is the color of veggie?

4

He's kind of tall and a little bit lean, completely silly, and cucumber-green.
LARRY THE CUCUMBER!

He's mostly round and not too tall . . . tomato-red is his color overall.

BOB THE TOMATO!

5

Word Search

Find and circle all your VeggieTales friends' names in the word search below.

P	E	R	C	Y	E	Q	P	G	I	G	E
H	S	Y	F	I	W	V	A	T	B	C	D
I	T	M	N	Z	D	U	G	N	M	J	U
L	I	N	S	X	G	K	R	U	K	U	A
L	A	R	C	H	I	B	A	L	D	N	L
I	A	Z	O	B	L	O	P	R	O	I	C
P	R	Q	O	S	P	B	E	M	N	O	N
E	U	M	T	J	Y	M	M	I	J	R	A
S	A	T	E	E	S	T	H	E	R	Z	E
U	L	A	R	R	Y	V	L	N	B	O	J
F	N	E	M	R	N	E	Z	Z	E	R	T
R	O	P	Q	Y	W	B	W	S	T	O	L

MR. LUNT	**LARRY**	**ARCHIBALD**	**JERRY**
JEAN CLAUDE	**BOB**	**PA GRAPE**	**JIMMY**
PHILLIPE	**JUNIOR**	**PERCY**	**ESTHER**
MR. NEZZER	**LAURA**	**SCOOTER**	**ANNIE**

6

You have to admit, they're asparagus-green, and would you believe they share the same genes? **MOM, DAD,** and **JUNIOR ASPARAGUS!**

Even in all of her baseball gear, she's carrot-orange from ear to ear.

LAURA CARROT!

8

Mixin' Up the Colors!

Mix two crayon colors, listed in the boxes below, and find out what third color is made.

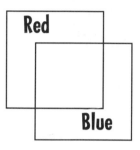

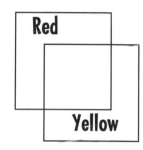

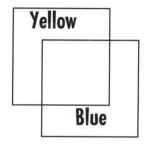

Red + Blue = _____

Red + Yellow = _____

Yellow + Blue = _____

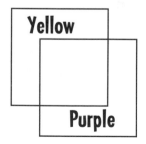

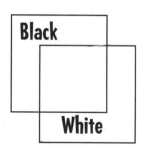

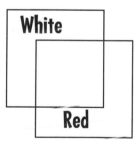

Yellow + Purple = _____

Black + White = _____

White + Red = _____

This grape-green fellow often plays a pirate. His hat is humongous, but that's how he likes it! **PA GRAPE!**

She's blueberry-blue, that much is true . . . but in this disguise,
can you guess who? **MADAME BLUEBERRY!**

Which Is Different?

Circle the picture that's not the same as the other three.

They're so very French—*oui, oui*—and they're as green as peas can be.
JEAN CLAUDE and **PHILLIPE PEA!**

14

That's a really big hat this guy sits below! This mister is a shade of light gourd-yellow. **MR. LUNT!**

Color Matcher!

How well do you know the veggies?

Draw a line to match the name of each color to each picture.

Red

Green

Blue

Yellow

Orange

This tall, asparagus-green-looking guy usually wears a red bow tie.
ARCHIBALD ASPARAGUS!

16

This orange carrot is the one to call, because doing his duty isn't a bother at all!
SCOOTER!

Who's There?

Connect the dots to see a little, green veggie.

1
2
10
3
9
8
5
7
6

18

This tall, green veggie wears a very pretty dress. Who could she be?
Can you make a guess? **ESTHER!**

19

He's a bright yellow gourd as anyone can see. He can often be found with his good friend Jimmy. **JERRY GOURD!**

Hide-and-Seek

Color the spaces with dots in them red to find out who's hiding in the picture.

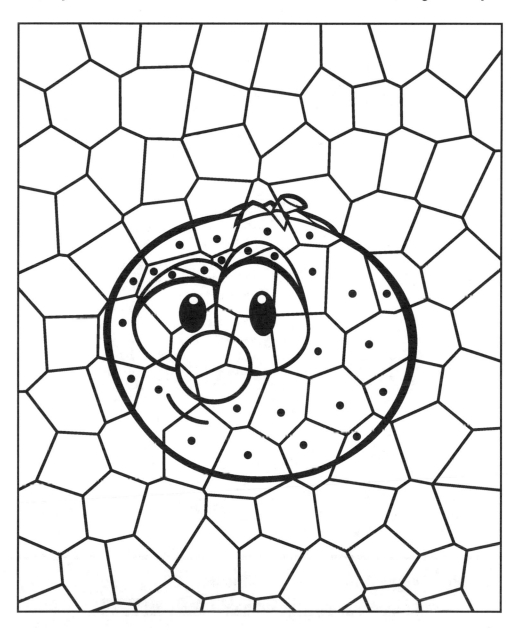

This zucchini-green veggie looks a little like Larry . . . but he's a tiny bit bigger, and a little bit hairy! **MR. NEZZER!**

Everyone knows that Jerry's his friend, and he's all gourd-orange from end to end. **JIMMY GOURD!**

23

Absent

Draw another green character on this page.

24

If you're not careful, you'll miss this peewee. He's small and green . . .
and actually a pea! **PERCY PEA!**

This petite preteen is scallion-green. She's grateful for pie, the sky, and everything! **ANNIE!**

26

What Color Am I?

Fill in each character's color in the crossword puzzle.

Across
1. Laura
3. Mr. Lunt
5. Bob

Down
2. Larry
4. Madame Blueberry

27

Maybe you missed it if you happened to blink . . .

but the colors of veggies are unique and distinct!

Color by Numbers!

Color in the picture using the colors below for each numbered section.

1 = Red   2 = Green   3 = Yellow
4 = Orange   5 = Blue

Answer Key

page 6

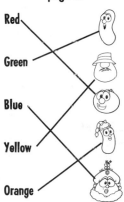

page 9

Red + Blue = Purple

Red + Yellow = Orange

Yellow + Blue = Green

Yellow + Purple = Brown

Black + White = Gray

White + Red = Pink

page 12

page 15

Red

Green

Blue

Yellow

Orange

page 18: Junior!

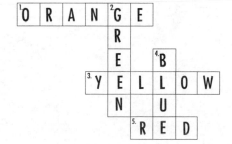

page 24:

Possible answers:
Annie, Archibald, Esther, Jean Claude,
Larry, Mr. Nezzer, Pa Grape,
Percy Pea, Phillipe Pea

page 27

```
¹O R A N ²G E
          R
          E      ⁴B
      ³·Y E L L O W
          N      U
            ⁵·R E D
```

31

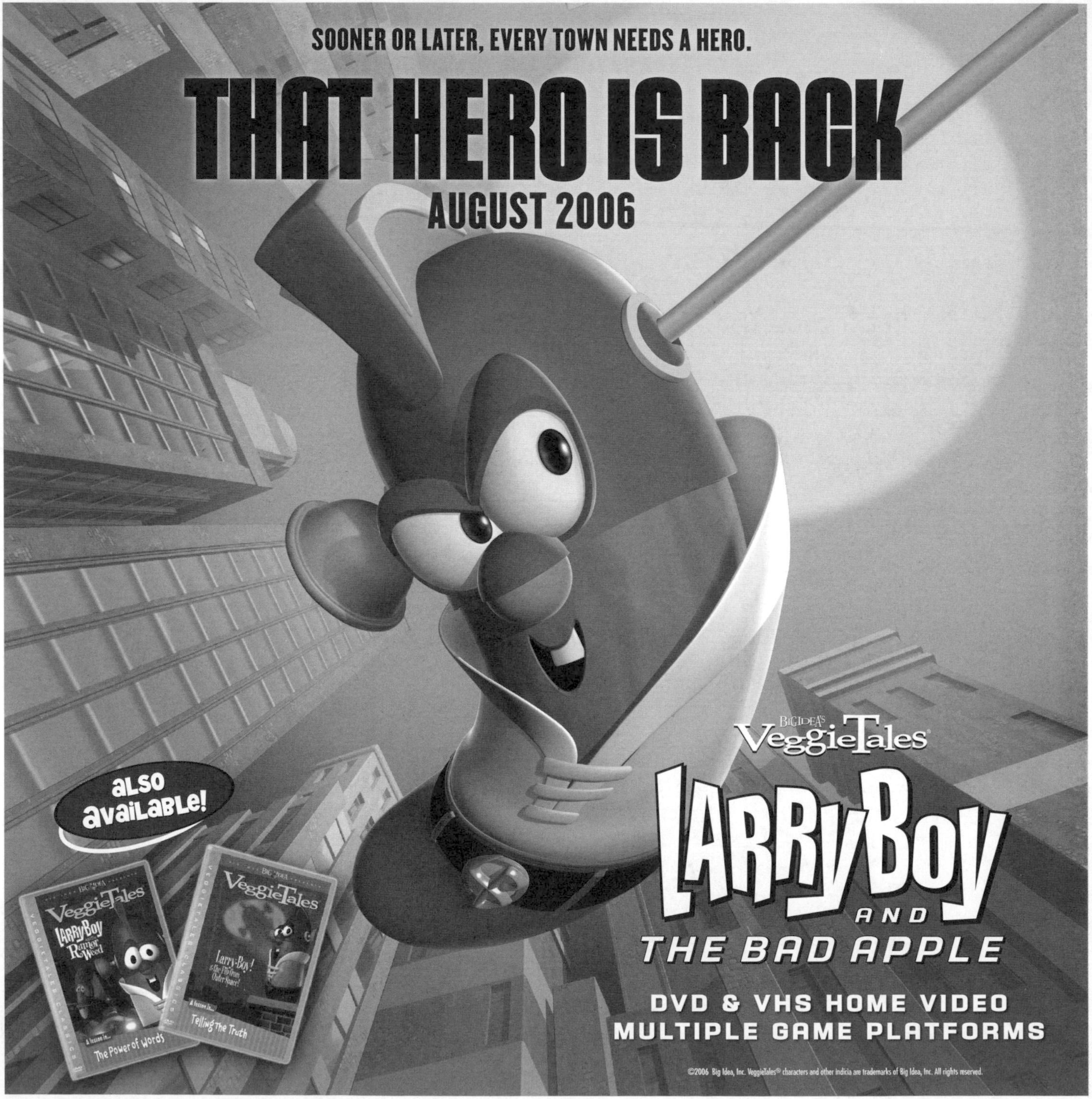
SOONER OR LATER, EVERY TOWN NEEDS A HERO.
THAT HERO IS BACK
AUGUST 2006
also available!
VeggieTales
The Power of Words
VeggieTales
Telling the Truth
BIG IDEA'S VeggieTales
LARRYBOY AND THE BAD APPLE
DVD & VHS HOME VIDEO
MULTIPLE GAME PLATFORMS
©2006 Big Idea, Inc. VeggieTales® characters and other indicia are trademarks of Big Idea, Inc. All rights reserved.